ZIGZAG

Written by Robert D. San Souci
Illustrated by Stefan Czernecki

AUGUST HOUSE
Little folk

With many thanks to Mahdi Heidari, Terry Clark and Tiffany Stone
for their help in the preparation of this book.

Copyright © 2005 Robert San Souci
Illustrations copyright © 2005 by Stefan Czernecki

Published 2005 by August House LittleFolk, P.O. Box 3223, Little Rock, Arkansas 72203 501-372-5450
www.augusthouse.com

Published simultaneously in Canada by TRADEWIND BOOKS, LTD.

Book design by Doug McCaffry

The text of this book is set in Bembo.

10 9 8 7 6 5 4 3 2 1

LIBRARY OF CONGRESS CATALOGING-IN-PUBLICATION DATA
. . . .
San Souci, Robert D.
Zigzag / Robert D. San Souci ; illustrated by Stefan Czernecki.
          p.   cm.
Summary: With some help from a group of field mice, an odd-looking doll—named
Zigzag for his crooked mouth—searches for a child to love him.
ISBN 0-87483-764-2 (alk. paper)
[1. Dolls—Fiction. 2. Mice—Fiction. 3. Toys—Fiction.] I. Czernecki, Stefan, ill. II. Title.
PZ7.S1947Zig 2005
[E]—dc22   2005041067
. . . .

Color Separations by Brideport Graphics • Manufactured in Korea

The paper used in this publication meets the minimum requirements of the American National Standards
for Information Sciences - Permanence of Paper for Printed Library Materials, ANSI.48-1984

*To Svea Leventon
(and her parents, Cassie and Ken)— R.S.S.*

For Tiffany Stone— S.C.

"I'll name you Zigzag," said the dollmaker, as she finished sewing her new doll's mouth.

He was made of scraps. He was odd-looking, with spiky hair, patchwork clothes and tiny wings.

His zigzag mouth made him look sad, but something about him made the dollmaker smile.

The dollmaker put Zigzag on a shelf with the other dolls.

"Some child will love you," she told him. Then she put out the lights and closed her shop for the night.

That night the toys woke and stared
at the strange new doll.

"What mother would buy that awful
thing for her child?" wondered the lion.

The penguin agreed, "He'd give a little
boy or girl nightmares."

"I'm just special," Zigzag insisted.

"You're just ugly," the elephant snorted.

The other dolls began to laugh. "Ha! Ha! Ho! Ho!"

"Hee-hee-hee!" they roared, "You are so very UG-ly!"

The bunnies began to chant,
"Squeeze him out!
Squeeze him out!
Squeeze him out!"

All the dolls helped the bunnies
push Zigzag off the shelf.

As Zigzag fell, he tumbled past the
stuffed satin teapots *thumpty-thump*
right into the wastebasket.

When the dollmaker opened her shop
the next morning, all the dolls sat silently
as if nothing had happened.

Then she emptied the wastebasket into
the dustbin behind her shop.

That night, Zigzag struggled out of the dustbin.

Some child will love me, he told himself, remembering what the dollmaker had said.

While crossing the park, he heard, "Who? Who? Who?" from a treetop.

"I'm Zigzag," he answered.

A hunting owl swooped down and carried Zigzag high into the sky, thinking he might make a good dinner.

But when he realized Zigzag was a doll, he let him go.

Zigzag fell into a meadow of thick, soft grass. As he brushed himself off, whispery voices asked, "Who are you?"

"I'm Zigzag," he said.

Three field mice crept out of the grass.

"Why are you here?" they asked.

"I'm looking for a child to love me," he said.

The mice took him to wise Papa Mouse.

"I want to find a child to love me," Zigzag told him.

"Our cousins live in a house nearby," said Papa. "The little girl there feeds them bread and cheese."

"She sounds just like the kind of child I'm looking for," said Zigzag.

"My children will take you there," said Papa Mouse. "But watch out for the hungry owl."

So off they went.

Suddenly the owl flew down to see what made the meadow grass move.

Up jumped Zigzag, shouting, "Remember me?"

"Silly doll," the owl screeched. And he flew away without ever seeing the little mice.

The windows of the little girl's house were dark. Everyone was asleep.

With the mice's help, Zigzag climbed the steps to the front porch.

"Do you think the little girl will like me?" he asked.

"She will love you," the mice promised.

The next morning, the little girl found Zigzag sitting on her porch. She hugged him and took him to her room. There, she sat him at a toy table, served him cups of tea and told him funny stories.

I've finally found someone to love me, Zigzag thought.

And his sad-looking zigzag mouth turned into a smile of joy.